To Richard

Storms in Jars

by

E.J. More

First published as an eBook in 2012.
First published in paperback in 2013.

Copyright © 2012 E.J. More

The right of E.J.More to be identified as the author of this work has been asserted by her in accordance with the Copyright, Designs and Patents Act 1988.

All rights reserved. This publication may not be reproduced, stored in a retrieval system or transmitted, in any form or by any means, electronic, mechanical, photocopying, recording or otherwise, without the prior permission of the author.

All characters in this publication are fictitious. Any resemblance to real persons, living or dead, is purely coincidental.

Contact: elijo.more@googlemail.com
Or visit the Storms in Jars Facebook page.

Cover design by Cheryl Casey Ramirez
www.CCRBookCoverDesign.com

For my boys

Special thanks to Jennifer Floutier

(Or as I like to call her, *Mum*)

Table of Contents

Smoke 1

Milton Hobbs and the Price of Serenity 11

Other Beryl 35

Post 54

Kimmy's Not Welcome Here Anymore 67

Smoke

It was two days since the creature had woken hungry. Friday evenings were the worst of times to rise. With the workers gone for the weekend food was scarce. It had resisted the urge to go in search of a domestic. They buffed and polished through the early hours, bringing the building's vast network of hallways and open-plan offices to a high shine. That kept them healthy and it had no desire to chase one down, let alone eat one. Too much effort, too risky, *too bland*.

Soon the sun would be up and the workers would return, bringing with them the delicious odour of cancer and rot. Then it would be glad it had waited. That first taste would be all the sweeter. It sank back in the dark and began to drool.

But its edge was gone, the need to feed now motivated only by hunger, not appetite. How many times had it woken? It felt like thousands. The world was a different place now. Driven from its habitat time and again, forced to find new hunting grounds, new food sources, it grew weary of the fight to exist.

Many years ago it had stumbled upon this place, one of the last remaining safe havens. A clandestine meeting place made possible only by a dinosaur company boss, as pig-headed as he was old-school. This was a man who loved a good cigar and wasn't about to let some *hoky-coky* government tell him how he could and couldn't run his business, smoke room included.

So here the creature stayed, blessed and cursed, unable to help but feel trapped by the fact that it had nowhere else to go. How it longed for another with which to share its prey, to rest with, to wake with. Instead it lived, as it had for the better part of a lifetime, with only the persistent ache of loneliness as its companion.

It hadn't seen one of its own kind since the global tobacco ban, a black day indeed. In the years that followed those that hadn't starved to death crawled back down below, beaten and desperate. It often wondered if it was the last to remain on the surface, but still it had no desire to return to the cavernous netherworld of its homeland. It would die here first.

Its nostrils twitched as it sniffed the air, sensing a variation. It inched forward a little for a better view of the hatch. In the room below a door creaked open, a moment later the sound of a switch; streams of light shooting upwards through the grid, projecting a geometric pattern on the roof above. Then footsteps and the shuffle of a chair as someone sat down.

The creature crouched silently in the ceiling space, unseen as it leaned over the hatch, its face a distorted collage of shadows. Before it even laid eyes on him it knew the human by smell, it knew all of them by smell. And this particular one was Fat Barry from payroll.

The man lit up a cigarette, sucking in hard and savouring the first lungful. It was still early so Fat

Barry hadn't yet begun to sweat, but by lunchtime he would have to change his shirt. He did this every day. Stinky Fat Barry from payroll, *Barry Two-Shirts*.

Life was not good for Barry. His spiteful co-workers talked about him when he wasn't there, mimicked his facial expressions, or left the smoke room en masse as he arrived. This only served to confirm what the creature had known forever, that humans were a cruel race, a selfish breed, one that deserved nothing other than to be feasted upon.

But not Barry, who, by some quirk of genetics, had managed to escape the onset of disease. Despite his size, his illicit nicotine addiction, there was nothing about his smell that indicated he would be suitable prey. And the creature was glad, it liked Barry, it knew his pain. But more to the point it knew what hard work a body like that would be, logistically speaking.

It had often needed to break bones, shoulders, hips, ribs, to get the humans up through the hatch. But Barry, well Barry was enormous, and the creature didn't relish the idea of trying to drag that amount of flesh up into the ceiling space. At its age it wasn't sure it could. So for lots of reasons Barry was off the menu. And as he stubbed out his cigarette and headed for the door the creature found itself a little sad to see him go.

It glanced around, a haze of smoke now creeping up through the grid. The light from the hatch didn't reach far so, for the most part, the huge expanse the creature considered its home was in darkness. The breeze block walls and supporting steel structures chilled the air, and it wished it hadn't discarded the skin of its last kill so quickly.

A few of the other hatches now glowed brightly in the distance, offices springing back to life, workers returning to their seemingly pointless jobs. But it didn't venture towards those. The only hatch it was interested in was here. So here it sat, patiently waiting, its eyes fixed on the grid that was its gateway to the room below.

An endless trail of humans came and went, breathing in their toxic fumes, poisoning their bodies. They were all dying, every last one, but they were too busy to even notice. Some were closer to death than they realised while others still had a ways to go, but all were on the spectrum.

It watched and listened as they chattered about everything and nothing; a series of meaningless ten minute interludes breaking up an equally meaningless day. How small they seemed to the creature now, their lives so disconnected. Forced to work like ants in a farm just to validate their existence. It might have pitied them, if it weren't their own doing.

It was waiting for a ripe one and knew just which one would do. The traffic slowed and the creature closed its eyes, but it sat up as it heard the clip-clop of heels from the corridor. The door creaked open once more and it instantly identified the scent, its mouth juicing up at the promise of food. Maybe this time it would be enough to fill the emptiness, to satisfy the ache. It lived in hope.

Lorna, PA to the boss, held a menthol cigarette between perfectly manicured fingers. She had spent her twenties sleeping her way up the career ladder and the creature could smell the old man on her now. She would often start his day that way.

'Gotta look after The Chief,' she'd say, ever so slightly repulsed by herself.

She was pale and on the unhealthy side of slim, her hair pulled up into a bun. She wanted so badly to feel professional, to feel clean. But lately her complexion had taken on a more pallid hue, the bony prominences of her face no longer striking in an attractive way. The youth she relied on so heavily now resided elsewhere, leaving not a lot else besides.

She spoke quietly into her mobile while the creature waited, biding its time, choosing its moment. It could smell the tumour the woman had yet to find, and the aroma of it made its heart race.

The creature leaned in towards the hatch, curling its claws beneath the edges of the grate, quietly and carefully levering it out of position. Its mouth formed a snarl, its jagged teeth instinctively bared. It was so hungry now, and the moment was close.

The growth sat in her left breast, deep in the tissue, where it was slowly turning the flesh inside black.

Within her lungs the disease had metastasised. Tiny cancerous spots, mere pinpricks, speckled the lining of the alveoli, growing fractionally bigger each day.

The creature studied the prey, its body coiled in anticipation. She was ripe for the taking, so very ripe. It had shown great patience and in a moment it would claim its reward, devour her piece by piece. Thankfully there would be no fight with this one, no struggle. It took a few slow, shallow breaths and it was ready. But then, as it braced itself to drop down through the hatch a noise close by made it stop and turn.

It took a moment for its eyes to adjust but then it saw it. A few metres away, only just visible in the shadows: a creature much like itself. They briefly sized each other up before the second creature tentatively moved forwards, out of the gloom.

The first creature's eyes filled with tears. *A companion. At last, a companion. To share my prey with, to rest with, to wake with. Yes, yes…*

But as the second creature approached it became clear it was no companion. It was younger and stronger, and it wasn't in the market to share. Drool dripped from its mouth as it bared its teeth in a predatory display. It was hungry and could smell disease. Not just from below but from the weak and aged body of the one in front of it. The new creature wanted the hunting ground for its own and would take it with ease. But first it wanted to feed.

The woman in the smoke room extinguished her cigarette and trotted back to work, unaware of the danger above, *or within*. While the old creature slumped slowly to the floor, a blanket of calm replacing the emptiness it had known so long. It had been here before, so it saw how all this would end.

Many years ago it too had arrived at this place, young and insatiable, eager to steal from its predecessor. Now it was the turn of another, and that was how it had to be. Only when it felt the burn of razor teeth sinking deep into its neck did the old creature speak the first words it had uttered in decades.

'Thank-you,' it said, closing its eyes, its ragged voice a mere whisper in the darkness. It slowly bowed its head, knowing it could do no more.

Milton Hobbs and the Price of Serenity

I'm sitting in my car, engine running, forearms tingling from the chill of the air-con. I'd like very much not to be here. I watch the same people trudge into the church hall I see every Thursday evening, and some new faces I think. Poor bastards, Day One stinks like the mother of all turds. I look for Dougie but I don't see him. Perhaps he went in already. I might toss a coin, ask fate the question. Not that I'll go with the wrong answer. I'm coming to hate Thursdays.

One minute past seven and they close the doors. I guess I should go in now. Don't want to be the prick that interrupts the main share. I think Gordon's talking tonight, but it makes no odds. They all sound the same to me now, their stories interchangeable. Bunch of whiners, makes me want a drink.

I haul myself out of the car, close the door and secure it with a click. The lights flash but I check it's locked anyway, can't be too careful. This area of town really is *Shitsville*, and if I come out after the meeting and find my car gone I swear to fucking God I'll kill somebody.

I cross the road thinking I might just keep walking. I could always tell Tess what she wants to hear when I get home. She'd never know. I'm a very good liar. But then I'm at the door, so I decide I might as well get it over with, and I reach for the handle.

I'm about to go in but a voice makes me stop.

'Hey Milt, how's it going?' the voice says.

I turn but see no-one.

'Hello?' I say. 'Is someone there?'

Out from behind a bush walks a man, tall and lean, dressed in a smart, dark business suit. I don't recognise him but he seems to know me. He walks over with a smile. I speed-search my memory but can't place him. Due to our whereabouts I assume he's a drunk, like the others, but a well turned-out one at that. I smile back, to hide my awkward embarrassment at not remembering his name. Or face for that matter.

'Looking good, Milt,' the man says. 'Six months on the wagon really has worked wonders. How's that lovely wife of yours? Everything back on track now I hope.'

'Yes, still married,' I say, wondering how the man knows things about my relationship. 'Ten years next June. And you; how's your other half?' I'm clutching at straws but hiding it well. After so many blackouts I have tactics.

The man explodes into raucous laughter. I am suddenly uncomfortable, but not sure why. I'm starting to think there is something familiar about him, though it's too distant in my mind right now.

'Oh, Milton,' he says, when the laughter stops, 'you know very well I'm a confirmed bachelor. No woman has what it takes to handle me.'

He winks, and there's that uncomfortable feeling again.

'So how are things at work Milt? Last time we met, if I remember rightly, it was looking grim. But I gather things have improved in that department too?' He looks over the road at my BMW, then back at me.

I don't like this man, I decide.

'Good thanks. Anyway I'd better get inside, they're about to start, and you know what Bill's like about latecomers. Nice seeing you again.' I try to sound casual. All I want to do is leave, get away from the stranger.

He is still smiling at me, and his gaze is too intense.

'Okay then,' he says as I open the door. 'Catch up with you soon.'

Our eyes lock for a beat longer than I'm happy with, and when I turn to go in I can still feel him watching. I walk into the meeting. Bill glares at me from behind the top table, but I don't care. I'm just glad to be surrounded by this familiar gang of losers. It feels safe. Gordon's sharing his little heart out so barely even notices me come in. A few of the others give me a nod as I cross the room. I sit down and realise my pulse is batting along at a rate of knots. I close my eyes and breathe.

During the break some of the others go outside for a cigarette. They ask me if I'm going too but I say no, I'm trying to cut down. They don't question me further, like I said, I'm a good liar. Instead I eat cheap biscuits, drink tea and make idle chatter with the drunks. I can relate to their problems, I used to drink, but I'm not like them. Not really. I pity them, holding hands and thanking the almighty for showing them the way. Happy-clappy bastards, how deluded they all are, how pathetic. Just grow a spine for fuck's sake.

I sit through the second half as a number of others pipe up to share their misery with the group. *Who is this helping*, I wonder, *them or me*? Soul leeches, all of them. I disguise a yawn. One woman's recollection of how she *really* wanted a drink this morning is met with sympathetic nods. *Jeee-zuss*, I think, looking up at the clock. My arms are folded and my foot is jiggling. I realise this makes me look impatient so I make it stop.

At last it's over and I'm the first to the door. But before I can get out Bill calls over to me.

Dammit. I turn back and walk across to the top table.

'Hi there Milton,' he says. 'I'm glad you're here. I've been meaning to ask you something.'

I know what's coming but I hope I'm wrong. I'm not.

'I don't suppose you could do the main share on Saturday? Dave was gonna do it only he's gone AWOL, which leaves us without a speaker. What do you think? Help an old man out, would you?'

'Sorry, Bill,' I say. 'Bad timing. I'm away all weekend, or else I would. Sorry mate.' I'm lying. Again.

'That's okay,' Bill says, 'maybe next time then.'

He's a good man, Bill. I feel a twinge of guilt, but not enough to tell the truth. I notice Dougie clearing the cups away on the other side of the room, and raise my hand to signal I'm leaving. He waves back with a cheery smile. I wonder if I should help him but decide not to. I want out of here. I'm done with church halls.

By the time I'm outside the others have scattered in all directions. Being August it's still light. The warm breeze and cut-grass-and-pollen air makes me want to sit in a beer garden. My taste buds are craving cold lager and salted crisps. I'm more than a tad tempted by this idea when I hear the man in the suit. He's been waiting.

'So how'd it go in there?' he says.

I turn to find him stood right behind me. I wonder how he managed to get so close without me hearing, but then he speaks again.

'Not doing it for you, is it?'

'I'm sorry, do I know you?' I ask. I am no longer interested in maintaining the charade.

'Indeed you do, Milton. But the last time we met you were in a rather bad way, so I'll forgive you for not remembering. I'll refresh your memory shall I? We had an arrangement, Milton, a very generous one on my part I think.'

'Arrangement? What are you talking about?'

'I promised you a six month trial and that's exactly what you've had. Now I've returned, as I said I would, to offer you the full package.'

'Six month trial of what?'

'Sobriety, dear boy, sobriety. Last time I saw you your life was in the gutter. You begged me for help, *begged* Milton. Don't you remember? And haven't I helped you? Isn't your life so much better now? You can't tell me you want to go back to how things were?'

I stare at the man. He is taller than me and I find this intimidating. The more I look at him the more I feel I should remember him, as if it's important that I remember him, but my memory fails me yet again.

'Are you trying to take credit for me quitting the drink?' I say. 'Because if you are that's the most ridiculous thing I've ever heard. I stopped drinking without anyone else's help. So whatever arrangement you think we had it's off. You got that? Now if you know what's good for you, you'll leave me alone.'

'Places to be have we?' the man calls out, as I walk towards my car. 'Like a nice beer garden? For a fresh pint of cool lager…?'

I stop in the middle of the road.

'…Icy rivers of condensation trickling down the glass; that first sip through the froth, smooth and refreshing. Heck, perhaps even a packet of salted crisps on the side. Let's go all out shall we Milt, *whattaya* say?'

I turn to face him.

'You know what you are, Milton?' he says, his voice suddenly full of contempt. 'You're what's known in the trade as a Dry Drunk. You may be sober in body, but up here,' he taps his finger to his temple, 'well, that's a different story. I bet it's been a long six months, hasn't it Milt? Meeting after dull old meeting. Squash after Coke after juice. When all you really want is to crack open a cold one from the fridge, maybe pour a nice tall G and T over ice on a warm summer's day. Well there is an alternative, Milt, there's always an alternative. And I can help you with that, if you'd like me to.'

I look at him for a moment. I don't know what he means by alternative but I'm pretty sure I don't like the sound of it. I realise I've been stood in the road awhile now and wonder if any cars have gone by. If they have I didn't notice. The man has my full attention and he's smiling at me again, awaiting a response. So I respond.

'Fuck you,' I say.

'Okay,' he replies, 'your choice.'

And with that our conversation is over. I hear the door of the meeting hall open and see Dougie and Bill walk out onto the street. They are laughing about something and I'm very glad to see them.

'Catch up with you soon,' the man says as he heads off down the pavement. I watch him till he turns the corner and disappears out of view.

'You alright there Milt?' Dougie looks at me, concerned.

'Yes, I'm fine, just... fine. Thanks Dougie. I'll see you next week.' Two more lies, in quick succession this time. I'm not fine. In fact I'm shaking. And I've no intention of returning next week, the hell with that.

I get in my car and floor it home. I just want to see Tess, to know everything's going to be alright. When I walk in the house and see her standing there I throw my arms around her and I hold her so close I can feel her body pressed up against mine.

I hold her like that for a long time, until I'm no longer thinking about the church hall, or the man, or how frightened he made me feel. Tess doesn't ask about the meeting, instead she strokes my face and kisses my cheek. I take her by the hand and lead her upstairs where we make love.

Thank God for her, I think as I look down at my beautiful wife, her legs entwined with mine, her arms pulling me in to her. As I ejaculate I kiss her hard on the mouth, thrusting myself deep inside, wishing I could hold onto the bliss just a moment longer.

I watch her as she drops off to sleep beside me. I think of everything I put her through, how she forgave me, and how she can still find it within herself to love me. *Thank God for her.*

By the weekend I have all but forgotten the man in the suit. It's Saturday and we're at a barbeque. These are Tess's work friends, and while she goes off to socialise I'm left alone to mingle with a garden full of strangers.

I find myself drawn to the coals, and I watch as the man I assume to be the host flips sizzling burgers and rotates blackened sausages a quarter turn each. The sun is beating down and I feel conspicuous in the Hawaiian shirt Tess got me for our last holiday. Conversations go on around me but I feel like an outsider, unable to offer anything of interest to these people.

Next to the barbeque is a long, foldaway table, covered with a chequered cloth, and on the table are a few dozen cans of bitter. Next to them are two cool boxes filled with ice, out of which poke an assortment of lager cans and crown-topped bottles. I'm suddenly very thirsty.

I look across the garden and see Tess deep in conversation. Whatever they're talking about she finds amusing as she's laughing in that natural, unaffected way that made me first fall in love with her.

'You look like a Stella man,' The Host says.

I look up to see him rummaging in one of the cool boxes. He pulls out a can of Stella Artois and hands it to me.

'There you go mate,' he says.

Such a cheerful guy, I think, and for a second I desperately envy him. This is a man who clearly has no issue with alcohol. Then I reach out and take the can.

'Cheers,' I say, 'that'll do nicely.'

I crack it open and take a long glug. It tastes good, so good I wonder how I could ever have given it up in the first place.

'Did you watch the big fight last night?' The Host says. I shake my head. 'Only I Sky-Plussed it. Some of us guys are gonna go in and watch it after. You're welcome to join us if you'd like. The more the merrier.'

'Wow, yeah,' I say, 'sounds great.'

He thinks we're bonding over sport; I think we're bonding because he has booze. Either way, it seems to be working for us both right now, and at last I'm starting to feel more at ease.

Tess comes rushing over, her face looks panicked. She pulls me away by the elbow, out of The Host's earshot.

'What do you think you're doing?' she whispers. I can't tell if her tone is concern or anger.

'It's fine,' I say. 'I'm just having the one. You can't expect me to come to a party and not enjoy myself, surely? And anyway, don't forget it's you that brought me here.' Just thought I'd get that one in. Cheap shot, I know. She lowers her eyes.

'But you promised.' For a second there I think she's going to cry but she keeps it together, for which I'm glad.

'It's all under control,' I say. 'Just you go and have fun with your friends. I'm okay here. Look,' I point at the barbeque. 'I'm even helping with the cooking. Man make fire.'

I grunt like a caveman but Tess isn't laughing. We look at each other for a moment and she eventually gives in and goes back to her colleagues on the other side of the garden. I don't speak to her again, except later, to gesticulate across the lawn that I'm going inside to watch the fight. She nods, and looks sad.

She'll be okay, I tell myself. I'm only having the one.

By the ding of the last bell I'm on my seventh can of Stella and The Host brings in a bottle of cognac, which suits me fine, I'm ready for something stronger. He pours generous measures but I can't help wishing he'd just leave me the bottle. I'm starting to feel like my old self again. I'm the centre of the universe here and my jokes are fucking hilarious.

I'm not sure where Tess is, she may have even gone home, but I'm in no rush. I'm having the time of my life. And besides, I can always make it up to her tomorrow.

I wake up and wonder why the pillow's wet. No, I'm lying on grass: a garden? A park? God help me, a roundabout? My eyes focus on metal legs and I recognise the structure above as the barbeque, now cold and dead, from the party. That makes sense. I roll over and notice my jeans are piss-wet through. I wonder if it rained, but then I see the moisture is concentrated around the crotch.

My mind goes into overdrive as I try to come up with an exit strategy. The sky is overcast, the summer sun of yesterday forgotten. I'm cold, not to mention hung-over. I try the back door, which by some miracle is unlocked, and creep across the kitchen to a pile of laundry in the corner.

I strip from the waist down, listening for movement from upstairs. Mercifully the house is silent so I unfold a pair of joggers from the pile, holding them up to my lower half for a size comparison. The Host seemed roughly my size and I'm relieved to find the trousers fit me perfectly.

I sneak out of the house, discarding my sodden jeans and boxers in the bin out back, and make my way unsteadily down the road, away from the scene of the crime. I tell myself I never have to see any of those people again and this comforts me, if only a little.

I'm not ready to face Tess yet so I go and sit on a bench in the park. If I felt conspicuous yesterday I feel positively freakish now. Dressed in my gaudy shirt and another man's jogging bottoms I'm a stinking, mismatched wreck. I need a shower. I need my wife. Fuck that, what I need is a drink.

I watch the world go by. A gaggle of expensive-looking mothers - the kind that look like they have croissants and espresso for breakfast – arrive with their designer Bugaboos and matching toddlers. They regard me with suspicion between swing pushes, but the threat of my presence is clearly too much and they quickly move on.

I see them whispering as they leave. I tell myself their opinions are of little consequencc; that they give their banker husbands blow-jobs in return for expensive trinkets. But it's no good, the shame that always follows a bender sneaks up on me, overwhelms me. It is crushing and oppressive and I want it gone.

I check my watch and work out the pubs open in less than an hour. Have I been sat here that long? I get up and walk. My feet take me to The Rose and Crown, a small place with real ale and low ceilings on the edge of town. I'm only sat on the wall a few minutes when I hear the clank of bolts, and the door opens.

'Morning,' the landlord says to me, long past being judgemental of the early-birds that frequent his establishment. They are, after all, his bread-and-butter trade.

I go inside with the intention of just having a small lager-shandy, something to take the edge off, *hair of the dog.* But it's evening time before I'm asked to leave, and I weave my way down the road towards home, and my beautiful Tess. I think I'm ready to apologise now, I just hope she's ready to listen.

I can't find my keys. They must've been in my jeans, I think, so I bang on the front door to our house. Tess appears, she's been crying. I badly want to hug her, but she looks at me with disgust.

'Damn you,' she says, and she turns to go upstairs.

I decide it's best if I give her some time, she's obviously a bit upset, so I stagger through to the lounge. And there, sat on my sofa, bold as brass, is the man in the suit.

'What the hell are you doing here?' I say, or try to say. 'Get the fuck out of my house.'

'Now, now, Milt,' he says, 'is that any way to greet an old friend? I'm here to help you, can't you see that? Are you ready to be helped now, Milton? Have you had quite enough yet? I think maybe you have. And Tessa, she definitely thinks you've had enough.'

'Stay away from my wife,' I say, but I need to sit down. Yes, I very definitely need to sit down.

The floor greets me with a thud and I realise I'm prone. My first thought when I'm down there, quite inappropriately, is that I'm glad we spent the extra money on the thick pile carpet. It made for a softer landing.

'Are you ready for an alternative, Milt? All you have to do is say yes and I can make it all better. You want that craving to go away don't you? Your obsession with the booze, you want to be free of it? Well I can do that for you, Milt, *the full package*. You just have to say it's what you want, and I'll fix everything.'

I think about what the man's saying. I don't understand it but at the same time it sounds like the best offer I've ever had. I can barely speak, or raise my head, but from somewhere I manage a weak yes.

'Do you want it… more than anything?' he asks, his face close to mine now.

'Yes,' I say again, as I start to sob.

The man leans over me and shakes my limp hand.

'Then we have a deal,' he says, and he leans in even closer. He puts his mouth next to my ear and whispers, and as he speaks I can smell his breath. It smells of dead things.

'Make the most of your last night with your wife,' he says, 'because tomorrow I will take her from you.'

I want to ask him to explain, to tell him that I've changed my mind, that I don't know what he means. But I can say none of those things. Instead I'm holding onto the floor as the room goes cyclonic, and a moment later I pass out.

I am woken by the sound of rain on the conservatory roof. It's light but only the sort of dull light a heavily clouded sky can muster. I didn't choke on my own vomit in the night, so that's good. Then I remember what the man in the suit said: *tomorrow I will take her from you*, and I spring to my feet.

My head thuds in protest at the sudden change of altitude, but I fly up the stairs regardless, swinging on the bannister to make a sharp left at the top. Our bedroom door is slightly ajar and I hurtle into it full pelt, sending it crashing against the wall.

'What the hell are you doing?' Tess mutters, rolling over in bed to look at me.

I'm panting. I want to grab her, to tell her I'm sorry, to keep her safe forever. But I don't think she's up for that just yet. Instead I go over to the window and draw back the curtains. My heart does a double-beat as I look down and see the man in the suit stood in our back garden. He's staring up at the window, smiling.

'We have to leave, *now*,' I say, and I grab my wife's hand, dragging her from under the duvet.

She puts up a fight but I'm stronger and she knows it. I nearly lose my footing on the stairs but we keep going, and soon we're in the hallway. I grab my spare car keys off the brass hook, not once easing my grip on Tessa's wrist, and then we're running down the front path.

'Get in the car,' I say, unlocking the doors with a click.

'I'm not going anywhere with you, you're still bloody…'

'For once in your life, Tessa,' I've had enough of this shit, 'will you do as I fucking say? GET. IN. THE. CAR. Please.'

I don't know what it was I said but it appears to have worked, and Tess, still in her nightie, climbs into the passenger seat with no further resistance. I run round to the driver's side and see the man walking around the house, into the front garden.

When I pull the car door shut I hit the central locking but this does nothing to calm me. I thank God, Jesus, and all the angels in heaven as the car starts first time, and I punch it into gear, slamming the accelerator pedal to the floor a fraction of a second later.

The wheels spin at first but then the tyres bite tarmac and we're moving. I see the man in the rear-view mirror moving away from us. He's still smiling, and I don't like it one bit.

We pick up speed as we head out of town, neither of us speaking a word. I can still see his face; smell his foul stinking breath; hear his voice whispering in my ear: *catch up with you soon…*

The junction comes out of nowhere.

Oh shit.

I think the words come from me. I stamp on the brake, too late. The last noise I hear is a scream and I know I'll hear it forever.

Then darkness.

I'm sitting in the quiet room, but it's far from quiet. I listen as one of the others opens up. He's having a breakthrough. *Good for him*, I think, as I stir my tea. His tears win him applause, and a reassuring rub of the shoulders from someone sat behind; a far cry from the behaviour that put them here in the first place.

I speak when it's my turn. The words I say, you could call them *lies*, are only the words I feel I ought to say, given the circumstances. I tell them I'm following the program, that it works for me and that it can work for them too, if they want it enough. This pleases them and, in a way, I'm glad.

I don't mention the man in the suit, or how he kept his side of the bargain. No-one believes me when I do, so I save my breath. Nor do I mention my dead wife or the woman and child that went under my car. I keep them inside, untouched by others, mine and mine alone. I talk in platitudes to maintain equilibrium, both in the room and myself; for now that's the best I can do.

I see Dougie from time to time, my one and only visitor. I ask him why he comes and he tells me it helps him in his recovery, that it's more for his own sake than mine. But I think it's because he's a decent man, a kind man, a better man than me. I look forward to his visits. For the brief time we spend together he makes me believe in salvation.

Other Beryl

'Are you still there, Detective?'

'I'm back, Mr Graseby. Sorry, I had to take a call on the other line. So you were saying you think your wife is an imposter?'

'Yes, an imposter, that's right. I know my Beryl, you see. You don't go being married to someone for forty-seven years and not notice when they've changed. And believe me, whoever that is back at the bungalow it sure as heck isn't Beryl.

My Beryl's a kind, gentle woman. She'd not swat a fly if she could avoid it. She bakes you know, the most wonderful light Victoria sponge you've ever had. I'll get her to do you one. Well, I would. But I can't. 'Cause it's not Beryl anymore. It's someone else. You have to help me. I don't want to die.'

'Okay okay, can we start at the beginning please, Mr Graseby? When exactly did you notice that your wife was acting, shall we say, out of character?'

'It was a couple of months ago, when she got back from the retreat. She works so hard, what with me being in the chair an' all. I thought she deserved a break. So I booked myself in for a bit of respite care, just a week, down at that new private place over by the park. I'd heard good reports about it so thought I'd give it a go.

And Beryl, well I booked her into one of those spa hotels, a really nice one, out in the sticks. All mud, massages and meditation. Just right for Beryl that, bit of pampering. Since my illness kicked in proper, I've got MS, did I mention that? Anyway, since it put me down for good she's spent her days wheeling me around, lifting me in and out of bed, on and off the lav. It's never-ending for the poor woman. So this was just a way of showing my appreciation. Of saying

'Beryl, you're a good 'un. Have this on me.' You know?

And it wasn't cheap, I can tell you. Have you ever been to one of those places, Detective? By God, if I had my time again I'd open a chain of *holistic healing centres*, or whatever they call themselves, and then I'd be sitting in a gold-plated wheelchair now, not this heap of NHS shite.

As it happens I'd got some vouchers through the door for this gaff, kind of why I chose it really, but even with fifty per cent off it still cost an arm and a leg. No pun intended.'

'Mr Graseby, I appreciate it must have taken you quite some effort to get here today, and I'm sure your time is every bit as valuable as ours…'

'Sorry, I'll get back to it. Yes, yes. So as I was saying we both got back off our jollies, but from the get-go I knew something wasn't right. She was quiet and didn't smile, not once, in the whole of our first evening together. Now that might not sound unusual to you, Detective but that just wasn't my Beryl. If you knew her you'd know she's one of the happiest people you're ever likely to meet. But this Beryl, well, this Beryl had a sour look on her face, like she'd eaten something rancid. Miserable as sin she was.

I asked her about the retreat but she just mumbled 'it was alright', or something like that. So I left it, thinking she just needed to sleep. But the next day the same thing: face like a smacked arse, and the next day, and the next. She still did what she had to do, she took care of me right enough, but there was no love there, no joy.

Can you imagine what that felt like, Detective? I thought I was losing her, that she'd had a taste of freedom and realised how pathetic and hard and thankless her life was with me, and that she'd decided she wanted out after all.'

'After all?'

'Yes. When I first got my diagnosis, we were both in our fifties back then, I gave Beryl a get out of jail free card. I said she was still young enough to start again and that she could leave and I would understand. That I wouldn't stand in her way. She deserved a better life than this, I said.

I think I went further than that even, practically pushed her away if I remember right. I didn't want her to feel trapped you see. Not Beryl, my beautiful, kind Beryl. She'd have given up her own legs if it'd meant I could walk again. But she didn't go, nor later, when the wheelchair became a permanent fixture. I tried to get her to leave then too, to leave or put me in a home or whatever. But again, she stayed. Bloody stubborn woman, even then she stayed.'

'So maybe you've hit the nail on the head there, Mr Graseby. Perhaps Beryl wanted to leave but didn't know how to say it? Resentments are often slow-burners. Sometimes these things take years to surface.'

'Oh, if only that's all it was. If she'd wanted to leave me I'd have sprung for cab fare, and she knew that, I can assure you. But no, as time's gone on she's not only been quiet but secretive too. We have a basement, Detective, downstairs, obviously. We only ever used it for storage before, old clothes, furniture and the like. But lately it's where Beryl's been spending most of her time.

Downstairs. You see? She knows I can't make it down those steps, and yet she spends hours down there, hours. And she won't tell me what she's been doing when she comes back up either. Sometimes I think I hear her talking to someone down there, but who I've no idea. We've never had secrets, Beryl and I, never. So I'd say that was out of character, wouldn't you, Detective?'

'Yes, Mr Graseby, that's as maybe. But people change all the time, develop new interests, hobbies. It doesn't make them imposters. It just means they're evolving. As human beings have a tendency to do. And it certainly doesn't mean that your life is in any danger.'

'I can see why you'd say that, Detective, and a few weeks ago I'd have agreed with you. But I'm not the only one to notice changes. A few of the old boys down the centre started saying things a while back about their other halves. I didn't pay much attention at the time. Well, you don't do you?

We all meet up a couple of times a week. That's Me, Frank, Terry and a few others, for a beer and a chat, like. A few of us are in wheelchairs. Some manage just with sticks. They're probably not that far off the chair too, truth be told, but they manage for now. One of the blokes has early-onset Parkinsons, poor sod. That's Gareth, he's the youngest of us lot. His wife left him a few months ago. It was sad at the time but now I'm thinking he was the lucky one.'

'And these men, you said they were noticing changes in their wives too?'

'Yes, that's right. In the beginning most of us thought it was a bit of a laugh to be honest. Like all the women were having a mid-life thing going on. But then Mick came to the centre one day, a few weeks ago it was, and he looked shit-scared out of his mind. He rambled on about Sheila, that's his missus, how Sheila was going to cut him into bits or something.

Well, we all thought he was having a breakdown, what with him only having a year to live an' all. It affects everyone different, you know, when they tell you the clock's ticking. Nothing surprises me anymore. But then he said about her eyes and that's when I realised he wasn't losing it. That's when I started to pay attention. I wanted to talk to him about it, in private like, tell him I believed him. But he was making a bit of a scene so the centre ambulanced him away quick smart, and that's the last we saw of him.

And he's not the only one. In the last month three others have disappeared from the group. Not a word of explanation, they just don't show up anymore. If that's a coincidence then I'm George Clooney.'

'What was it he said about his wife's eyes?'

'Ah well, I was getting to that. A strange thing happened, you see. My glasses went missing just after me and Beryl got back from our little break. The way I reckon it is she took them so I couldn't see her clearly enough to notice the changes. But I saw them alright. Subtle little things, the kinds of things only a husband might notice. Well more fool her. My vision's not so bad that I couldn't see her eyes were a different colour.'

'Her eyes were brown and now they're blue, that type of thing?'

'No, it was the whites of her eyes that were different. They just looked wrong. To use Mick's words, it was like there was something behind there that shouldn't have been. And in a darkened room, if she looked at you from a certain angle, you could almost see them shine. I know for a fact my Beryl's eyes never did that before. That's something I'd remember, don't you think, Detective?'

'I imagine so, Mr Graseby, yes.'

'And then there's her skin. She had the softest skin my Beryl, peaches and cream. Miss Inkley Nook 1963 she was. I couldn't believe my luck when she said she'd marry me. Beryl Braithwaite marrying me, can you imagine? Beautiful skin she had, beautiful. But this Beryl, well her skin's dry, and cold to the touch. She didn't think I'd notice that, but I did. I just never said anything. I wanted to figure it all out in my own head first. Safer that way, I thought. Shows what I know.

Then a couple of days ago I woke in the night, and she was kind of arched over me, her legs straddling me if you like. Not my Beryl at all, that. Even in our younger days, when I was a proper man, even in our prime Beryl was never the adventurous type. So to wake up and see her over me like that, well, it was a shock to say the least. But I didn't move. I didn't want her to know I was awake. Not sure why. Instinct I suppose.

Then I felt something wet on my upper arm. It was dark and it took me a moment but eventually I realised what it was. Beryl was working her way up from my elbow to my shoulder, slow and deliberate, like. She was licking me, Detective. No, that's the wrong word, she was *tasting* me.

She was moaning as she did it too, like it was sorting her out, good an' proper. It's been a long time since my Beryl made noises like that I can tell you, with me at least, so I just pretended to be asleep. I wouldn't have had the strength to push her off even if I'd tried. And when she'd finished she just rolled over and stared up at the ceiling, with her shiny eyes, just stared. Now if you try and tell me that's normal behaviour, Detective, I'll eat my socks.

So you see, whoever or whatever that is living in the bungalow it's not my Beryl. And I'm not going back there, 'cause I think tonight's the night she's planning on doing something. She came up from the basement smiling this morning. Creepy as hell it was. Then when she left for the shops she said she was going to make a special dinner tonight.'

'And that's bad because..?'

'Mushroom stroganoff, Detective, mushroom stroganoff. Don't you get it? I hate mushrooms. Beryl would know that, she's always known that. Not a single mushroom has snuck its way onto my plate in nearly four decades, so why now? No, tonight's the night. Something happened to her at that retreat, something's happening to all the wives, and now she wants to kill me and eat me, I just know it. Please, you have to help me.'

'Mr Graseby, I think perhaps your imagination has run away with you. I appreciate your illness has put a great deal of strain on you and your wife, but I honestly think the best thing for you both is if you just went home. I'm sure after a good sleep you'll feel a lot better, and things will seem a little less, shall we say, bleak?'

'Haven't you heard a word I've said? If I go to sleep that's probably when she'll get me. Or maybe she'll not even wait till then and just push my wheelchair right down the basement steps, with me in it. I won't let you send me back there. I know my life might not seem like much to you, Detective, but it's still my life, and I'm not ready to give it up just yet. I'm begging you. You have to protect me.'

'Okay, Mr Graseby. Look, we can order an ambulance to take you home and we can get someone to escort you to the door. It'll be no trouble I can assure you.'

'That won't help. She may look just like my Beryl, she may talk and play the part, but once she's got me alone that'll be that, I'm telling you. Your officers can do a little jig on the front porch and it won't make a bit of difference. She's going to kill me. Don't you get it? If you send me back there I'm a dead man.'

'On the contrary, Mr Graseby, I spoke to your wife only a few minutes ago. She sounded worried about you. Said you'd been acting strangely since coming back from the respite hospital, 'out of character' she said. She just wants you home safe, where she can take good care of you. What do you think? Hey, I'll even call that ambulance for you myself. We'll have you home in no time.'

'For the love of God, why won't you listen? She's not my wife. Please believe me. Please. I don't understand. How did she even know I was here?'

'Mr Graseby, you're holding fourteen people hostage at gunpoint. Things like that have a habit of making it onto the news. I don't suppose there are many people in the country who don't know exactly where you are right now. If you'll just put the gun down I can come into the building and we can talk about where we go from here. How does that sound?'

'I'm on the news?'

'Yes, Mr Graseby.'

'Then we have to warn people.'

'There is no *we*, Mr Graseby, you've created this situation and it's up to you to make the right choice now. You know what the right choice is don't you, Mr Graseby?'

'But the world needs to know. We're all in danger, can't you see? I know what they're planning. They're targeting the invalids, the weak, defenceless ones. The ones they reckon society can do without, won't notice are gone. They're disguising themselves as wives, as carers. They're hiding away in homes where they know nobody will go looking. They know the government won't come knocking for fear of having to do something. In fact that useless lot probably already know and are just not getting involved. Suits them to let us disappear off the face of the earth rather than live out our lives on benefits, I bet. It's extermination, can't you see that, Detective?'

'Mr Graseby, please...'

'But what then, Detective, when they've gobbled up all us resource wasters? Maybe they'll get a taste for something healthier, aim for a more able-bodied reward. Perhaps they'll disguise themselves as co-workers, teachers, parents. Maybe they have already.

Nobody will be safe, Detective, nobody. So you see we have to tell people, before it's too late.'

'You sound like a reasonably intelligent man, Mr Graseby, so it must have become apparent to you by now that there is very little chance of us letting you go home after this. Therefore it would seem to me that you have, in fact, achieved your goal, in part at least. If you release the hostages and give yourself up we'll take you into police custody where you'll be safe. Beryl won't be able to get to you in jail, Mr Graseby, that I can promise you.'

'I am well aware of that, Detective, but I'm afraid I can't come out just yet. Not while I've got one of them in here with me. So as long as I've got a gun to her head I'm stuck here. Do you understand?'

'One of them?'

'Yes, Detective, Mick's wife. She saw me at the counter. I couldn't risk her telling Beryl, so I knew what I had to do. I've kept my gun close the last few days, under my chair cushion, 'cause I thought my time might be up. I only came in the post office to draw out my savings, so I could do a runner, like. I can assure you this wasn't what I had in mind when I woke up this morning. So there we have it, Detective. Bit of a stale-mate, wouldn't you say?'

'Not really, Mr Graseby, no. You see we've been keeping a very close eye on you these last couple of months. We thought something like this might happen, so steps were put in place to prevent things getting out of hand. *Damage limitation* you could call it. I really do think it would be best for everyone if you just put down the gun now and came out.'

'What do you mean? Who's been keeping a close eye on me?'

'Why Beryl of course. She alerted us that you were on to her some time ago. You really are one of the smart ones, Mr Graseby. Well done. We like that.'

'I don't understand. Who are you? You can't do anything to me, not with the whole country watching. You wouldn't.'

'Oh dear, Mr Graseby, you didn't really think the world was interested in you and your small life did you? There are no cameras outside. There are no news people rushing to tell your story. It's just you and us and, please believe me when I say this, we will win here.'

'But you're forgetting I've got one of your lot in here with me. I'll shoot her in the face if you don't let me out right now.'

'Go on then, Mr Graseby, you do that. Let's just see what happens shall we?'

'Oh God.'

'Mr Graseby?'

'Yes?'

'You did it didn't you.'

'Yes.'

'And what happened?'

'Her face grew back.'

'Her face grew back, yes. It's like I said, Mr Graseby, damage limitation. So you see there's not much you can do now is there? Put the gun down and we can finish what we started. Surely that's better than the long slow death you would've had? Really we're doing you a favour, Mr Graseby, you should be thanking us.'

'Thank-you my back side. I wouldn't give you the flamin' pleasure. You and your bunch of freaky, shiny-eyed weirdoes can kiss my useless arse. If you think I'm gonna just sit here and let you finish me off you don't know me as well as you reckon you do. This is what I think of your favour; this is for my Beryl…'

'Mr Graseby? Mr Graseby, can you hear me?'

'He's shot himself in the head, Sir.'

'Yes, Briggs, I can see that on the monitor thank-you. Right, is the clean-up crew ready? Okay, let's get all those people out of there.'

'What do we tell them all, Sir?'

'Jesus, Briggs, use some initiative, boy. Tell them what you like, just make sure it's contained. Tell them it's one of those hidden camera shows. People believe anything if they think it's on the telly.'

'Yes Sir.'

'Hello? Is anybody there?'

'Ah, yes. Hello again, Mr Graseby. How are we feeling?'

'Is that you, Detective? I don't understand. I put the gun in my mouth, how could I miss?'

'You didn't miss, Mr Graseby. You're becoming one of us. Your wife started the process but you're not quite finished yet. Luckily you were far enough along that you could heal. Please come out now, Mr Graseby. Come out and we'll finish what we started. There's so much we have to tell you.

Oh, and, Mr Graseby, I think you'll find you won't be needing that chair.'

Post

At first Zachary thought he'd had a stroke just like his grandma. He remembered his grandma. He was propped up against the fridge with no idea how he'd got there. His mind swam in jumbled memories; some he knew, others he wasn't even sure were his own. He knew he felt no pain, which concerned him somewhat, so he moved his feet just to know that he could. For some reason he knew he should be afraid, but of what he couldn't say. How long had he been there? The details escaped him. But he knew his name was Zachary, of that he was fairly sure.

He rolled onto his front and found a way to stand. If it was a stroke he was glad his legs still worked. This was definitely his kitchen. He recognised the faces on the fridge. There was a picture of the man he thought he was, with a woman he thought he knew. They looked happy, close, smiling by a pool. He concentrated but it just wouldn't come. He reached up to touch the picture, as if the feel of the paper might release her identity to him, but still nothing.

He saw blood on his hand, old blood, congealed and dark, tracking down from his shirt cuff. He went to the sink. The tap dripped every other second, the bowl full. He dunked his hand in but couldn't remember how to wash so pulled it back out again, the blood-stained water trickling down his fingers, leaving dirty brown puddles on the lino.

He paid no attention to the mess as by now he'd noticed a small gold band on the windowsill. He reached for it and held it between his grubby, wet fingers. He studied the ring then turned back to the woman on the fridge.

My wife, he thought, *I have a wife*. And in a flash he remembered her.

They'd fought, more than once, and she'd left. The reasons were gone from his mind but the gut-wrench, the paralysing sadness remained. He remembered he hadn't wanted her to go, that he loved her, he remembered that much. Something had happened, something beyond their control. It was right there, on the peripheries. He was just missing it. Just.

Think, think, think. But his brain wouldn't comply.

He walked slowly through the house, leaving a trail of brown drips behind. He walked out the door and there in the street was the reality: bodies, everywhere. Not whole but blood-soaked, torn apart bodies. And yet he didn't feel shocked, or nauseated. Instead he walked out into the road and began to examine the corpses, searching for signs of life.

They had been there a while. Their skin was pale, green-tinged, their faces lifted and cured by the sun. Their fingers clawed at the ground, the sky, each other. Most of their skulls were smashed in, remnants of grey matter now crusted onto the asphalt. He thought it odd that there was no smell; something wasn't right about that. He might have seen one of the bodies move in the distance, he wasn't sure, either way he didn't investigate. He was trying to remember and that, for the moment, took up all his focus.

Had there been a war? No, it was too quick for that. A bell rang, quiet and distant, before sinking back into the cerebral swamp. He decided to find his wife, Ellen, *yes Ellen*. If he had survived then perhaps she had too. He had to try. They could make things work, he knew it.

He walked over to a car and remembered it as his. But he couldn't remember how to drive so abandoned that plan and set off on foot. He found he could only move slowly, his gait skewed. He wondered if he'd damaged his legs in the fall, but as he was still unable to recall the events prior to waking on the kitchen floor he struggled on. He walked in the direction of the M1. For some reason he knew to head south. Ellen would be south, though how he knew that he couldn't say.

We thought we were safe… across the water. The words came from nowhere; they felt like a memory and they filled him. He began to walk in sync with their rhythm, repeating them over and over again in his head.

He hauled one foot in front of the other until he finally reached the motorway. It seemed barren and endless after the smaller roads of the town. He looked up at the signs but couldn't make out what they said, so chose which ramp to go down purely on instinct. It reassured him that it felt like he'd been this way before.

It was dusk when he saw a small group of survivors eating at the roadside. They must have sensed his hunger as they allowed him to join them. No-one spoke, there was nothing to say, and when Zachary was done he resumed his journey, grateful for their hospitality.

Derbyshire: that would be his journey's end. Ellen would head for her parents place, he was sure. A cottage on a winding lane, isolated, its own well. Where better to go when the world's turned to shit? She was smart, and resourceful, and the more Zachary thought about it the more convinced he became that his wife was alive, that she had survived somehow.

His clothes felt loose. Despite his full belly the hunger remained. He kept walking, following the white lines, step after step after step. *Across the water…* it nagged at him for miles. *We thought we were safe across the water*. Every pace brought him closer, not only to Ellen but also the truth.

Zachary kept walking. He passed abandoned cars jammed together around bottle-necked junctions; the spaces between littered with putrefying limbs and hollowed-out torsos, mere scraps of what had once been known as people. The moon lit the black strip of road ahead and for the rest of the night, trudging onward, he thought only of Ellen.

The sun came up just as he got to the exit ramp. He'd been walking for nearly a full day but didn't feel tired. He was starving but pushed the thought away and kept going, up the ramp, across the grass verge and towards the village near his in-law's place.

He navigated his way through the streets and soon found himself at the turning. The lane stretched down and away from the main road, curling through the valley and toward the cottage. He glanced back and spotted a group of survivors huddled together in the road. He toyed with the idea of asking if they had food but decided to go in search of his wife first, he needed to know she was safe, so set off down the lane.

He approached the cottage and saw Ellen in the front garden, her hair pulled out of her face with a headscarf, her face pink and vital in the morning sun. He wanted to call out to her but he knew his voice was gone, completely, irrevocably. He didn't know how he knew, he just *knew*, so didn't even try. Instead he walked up the path towards her, in the same ambling fashion that had got him all this way.

Then, when he neared his wife, the movement drew her eye. Something in her expression he couldn't place. Was it surprise? Shock? Only natural, she must have presumed him dead. He continued towards her, raising his arms, her wedding ring in his grasp. But instead of running into his embrace she jumped to her feet and stumbled back, towards the cottage, away from him.

He didn't understand. They'd argued but surely they could get past that, make things work? It had to be worth a shot, he thought. They had both survived after all.

He stopped and watched his wife. She had her back to him now and was reaching into the storage box at the side of the cottage. When she spun round she looked angry and had armed herself with an axe. He reached out his hand once more, only this time he noticed the appearance of his skin, and it worried him.

It was pale, turgid, his fingers coated in great scabs of dried blood and sinew. For a moment he forgot about his wife as his gaze drifted from fingers to wrist, up his jacket sleeve, all the way to his shoulder. There he saw that the fabric had been ripped away, a great hunk of flesh torn out, his shoulder bone protruding emphatically. And yet he still felt no pain. Then he remembered the attack.

Ellen had wanted to leave for the relative safety of the countryside. He, on the other hand, had insisted they stay in their own home. That the danger would pass soon enough. She called him a *fucking idiot* and she left. By that afternoon it reached his front door. How he hated it when she was right.

He locked the place up and hid. But they knew he was there, the bastards, they knew, and before long they were banging on the door. He made a choice. They were slow, slow enough to outrun at a push, so he snuck out the back door to escape. But there was one out there too, and it grabbed him, clamping its fetid mouth around his shoulder. He managed to push it away, but not before a sizeable chunk of him went with it, and he staggered back into the kitchen, feeling foolish and afraid.

He knew he was in trouble. His shoulder pulsed out blood faster than his body could cope with and soon he dropped to the floor, taking up refuge against the fridge. Outside, the one out back hurled itself at the kitchen door, again and again, like a rabid dog on speed.

Zachary bled out right there on the kitchen floor. His dwindling circulation, his oxygen starved organs, finally giving way to the inevitable: a death, of sorts.

He looked up from his shoulder to see Ellen rushing towards him. She swung the axe above her head, before swooping it back in a downward arc. She took Zachary's outstretched arm off clean, at the elbow, and it thudded on the floor like a long, thin joint of pork.

He looked down at the arm lying on the dew-damp grass; it didn't look like his, and he'd barely felt it come off. But before he could ponder this further Ellen swung at him again, lower this time, taking his right leg out above the knee. She screamed as she swung, like some crazed Wimbledon finalist, fighting for her life in a winner-takes-all, Centre Court death-match.

With one leg gone his balance failed and Zachary fell over to the side. He wished he could tell Ellen how much he loved her, how sorry he was for letting her go. But his mouth didn't work, not for speaking anyway, so he only hoped she would cherish the good times they'd shared. They were happy then, he remembered.

He remembered it all now, and as she swung the axe one last time, taking aim on his skull, he held her wedding ring tight. She would find it, he thought, the ring. She would find it and she'd know that he came to find her. Despite everything he came to find her. And in some small way that made him happy. Then, with a splintering of sharpened steel on bone, he was gone, and the world became a slightly safer place.

Ellen dumped her husband's dismembered corpse in a shallow grave, before splashing it with paraffin and watching it burn. She'd loved him once but as the flames subsided she felt nothing. The body in the ground was not her Zachary and, when it was ash, she covered it with dirt and walked away. She scrubbed her hands in a bucket of rainwater, getting off every last rank, infectious smear, and strode up toward the cottage.

It saddened her to think her parents might be out there somewhere, macabre cadaverous puppets, like Zachary. She thought it was safe here once, hidden from the main road, a good distance from the village. But she was wrong. She would have to move on.

Tomorrow she would pack up her things and go in search of somewhere safe, somewhere far away.

She didn't notice as one of her feet fell upon a small band of gold in the grass, the weight of her jamming it down into the earth. But as she got to the doorway she hesitated, thinking for a moment about Zachary.

To make the journey here would have taken thought, memory, a sense of direction, and that simply wasn't possible. *The dead can't remember*, she told herself. *And they sure as hell can't navigate*. But he was here nonetheless.

She brushed away tears and cast a final glance across the garden before closing the door on it all. Tomorrow would come soon enough, but for tonight at least she would sleep, safe in the knowledge her twice dead husband would not return again.

Down the lane a large group of survivors, slow but determined, limped and shuffled towards the cottage. In the twilight they followed the intermittent streaks of blood left by the last man to walk this way. Shoes worn through, feet eviscerated by the road, Zachary's every step had left its mark and now guided a hungry new threat towards his wife.

Two of them knew the way better than most. They remembered every twist and bend, every tree, every pothole. They knew as they approached the brow of the next hill they would see a cottage in the distance, and then it would not be long. They knew the back door would give way with ease, and that a feast most likely awaited them. Two of the dead remembered this road, and for them it felt like going home.

Kimmy's Not Welcome Here Anymore

Kimmy was the type of friend your mother wouldn't have approved of. Mine certainly didn't. But it was only as I grew older, had babies of my own, that I understood why. Of course back then what my parents did or didn't want fell low on my list of concerns. If anything their damning opinion made her more exotic to my naïve eye. Besides, she was my best friend and, at fifteen, best friends outweigh just about everything.

That night I was house bound, the result of some inane argument not worthy of recall, so Kimmy threw sticks at my window. I tried to be quiet but the sash caught every few inches as I jerked it upward, and I thought, more than once, I'd been rumbled.

'Bloody fire hazard,' I muttered.

That was my dad's doing. I don't know why but he had a thing about fires.

'Always check for fire exits,' he'd say. 'Make sure you know your way out in an emergency.'

To which I would usually roll my eyes in dismay, mortified by my parents' very existence.

The window finally slid open. I knew something must have happened as Kimmy was on one of her highs, unable to stand still even for a moment. She always went that way. Something I only later came to recognise as a coping mechanism, the mask of someone damaged far beyond my adolescent comprehension. But this was 1989, a time when I knew nothing of such things, so I can't beat myself up about that now.

'Hey you,' she said, 'get your arse down here missy. It's time for fun, fun, fun.'

'I'm not allowed out,' I said.

'What's allowed got to do with it? Anyway, who says? *Mummy and Daddy*? What do they know? Jack shit is what. I need you. Come on, don't be boring.'

She knew I hated it when she used that word. *Boring*, it was a trigger she pressed whenever she wanted her own way.

'You coming or what?' she said, impatient as ever, her eyes a dark pit of mischief.

'Coming where?' I said.

'Does it matter?'

And of course it didn't. If ever there was a muse she was mine, and I already knew, before I'd even begun to climb out the window, that I was gone. With Kimmy there was never any doubt.

I listened for noise from outside my door but all was quiet. I quickly threw on my favourite dress; it was my favourite because Kimmy had once told me I looked *totally shagable* in it, and for some reason that mattered.

I didn't give my parents a second thought as I lowered myself down onto the garage roof. As I think back now there were so many moments I could've done the right thing. But we were young and irresponsible, in the purgatory of pre-adulthood, with nothing to do but stumble blindly on through the mistakes that should've shaped our futures. That did shape mine.

We walked and talked a while, about shoes, about school, about nothing in particular. If I'd known how the night would end I might have made those last few hours mean something, to suggest going somewhere else. Or maybe I wouldn't.

Kimmy wasn't one to be told. She was a storm in a jar, a wild thing constrained by the rules of others, and I don't suppose I could've changed anything at all, even if I'd tried. And besides, I'd be lying if I said I didn't get a buzz from being swept along by her. She was intoxicating.

She'd brought with her two bottles of Diamond White and a plan. We'd go into town and flirt our way into the loudest club we could find. She wanted to dance all night. *Dance the demons away*, she said.

'You think they'll let us in?' I said.

'Leave that to me. I know what I'm doing.'

And she did. True, she looked older than me, but it was more than that. She had a handle on her sexuality, a flair for manipulation beyond her years. Something I didn't grasp until much later, perhaps never did.

She had men figured out from the start, and they responded to her in a way that, at the time, I couldn't fully understand. But she understood. She knew it granted her power. And every powerful being needs a side-kick, so I guess I was hers.

'I'm glad we're out,' she said, 'my Dad's home tonight.'

That was all she said on the subject of her father, and I didn't bring it up again. I'd learned not to.

'Shit,' she said. 'Leg it.'

She grabbed my arm and we both ran as the bus came round the corner. It wasn't going to stop but Kimmy jumped into the road, giving the driver no choice. He nearly didn't let us on because of it. But she charmed him, like she charmed everyone, and soon we were sat on the top deck, drinking our cider, as the bus rolled on into town.

'You know I love you, don't you?' she said, as we were approaching the bus terminal.

I nodded but said nothing. Her words made my stomach lurch, and I began to feel the tingle that came whenever I thought of her. Or perhaps it was just the movement of the bus. Her eyes looked right into mine; there was something else she wanted to say. At least that's how it felt at the time.

'I hear Craig and Mandy broke up,' she said, looking out of the window. A clumsy change of subject but one I was glad of. Did she know what she did to me, what she did to everyone?

'I heard that too,' I said.

'Why don't you ask him out?' she was still facing the window, her tone indifferent.

'What do I need him for,' I said, 'when I've got you?'

Kimmy turned back to face me. She smiled and gave my hand a squeeze. But it wasn't a real smile, not a *Kimmy* smile, and I knew that, although she was my whole world, I would never quite be enough for her. I wasn't sure anyone would be enough for her.

And that made me feel bad; bad about myself and bad for her.

I remember back then a lot of how I felt depended on Kimmy, a mistake I've not made again.

Weekends in town were always busy. We walked down the high street with its bars and takeaway joints. The air hummed with anticipation. At nine o'clock it was still early, everyone looked happy, the fights and tears a few hours - and a few drinks - down the line.

I thought I knew where we were headed: the big club in the middle of town, and the current favourite amongst the locals. But when I turned to check with Kimmy I realised she was no longer at my side. I scanned the pedestrianized area but she was gone, so I began to double back.

A group of men jeered past me, stags in matching t-shirts, lively and half-cut. I moved away, a little afraid of their pack mentality. They seemed much older than me at the time, but with hindsight they must only have been in their early twenties, their good natured banter threatening to a teenage girl alone.

Somewhere in the distance a bottle smashed, or maybe a pint glass, followed by a rowdy cheer. The smell of hot dogs and fried onions wafted out from a kiosk on the corner, and dance music echoed from each pub and club I passed. I could put these things in a bottle; label it *Friday Night in Farsworth*. One day I would leave this place forever, but back then it was all I'd known since childhood.

I couldn't see Kimmy anywhere. The sky was dark now and the streets less welcoming. A chill hit me as I approached the sea front so I untied the cardigan from around my waist, slipping it on over my dress. I was about to make my way back to the bus terminal when I heard my name. Kimmy was shouting to me from down the street. She was standing at the entrance to an alleyway, frantically signalling me over.

'Where the hell did you go?' I said when I got to her. But she didn't reply. Instead she skipped off into the alley and, as always, I followed.

'Look,' she said, 'we should go in here.'

She pointed to a small doorway. Above which a sign read 'Disco Below', in scrolled neon. From somewhere beyond the door Barry Gibb sang *You Should be Dancing*, and the cobblestones beneath our feet pulsated to the beat.

The alley was empty, apart from us, and if I were feeling generous I'd have said the place looked like a lap dancing club. It made me nervous to be there, and all I really wanted was to get back to the main street, where all the people were.

I looked at the doorway then back at Kimmy.

'It's a bit dated,' I said.

'Retro,' she said. 'Come on, it'll be a laugh.'

She was swinging her hips to the music, with all the excitement of a toddler in a ball pool. She reached out and held my hands, pulling them back and forth, making my body move with hers. She raised her eyebrows in that *you-know-you-want-to* way and I knew then my view would count for nothing; that we might as well go in now, as she would convince me sooner or later anyway. She always did.

'Hello ladies. Will you be joining us tonight?'

We both looked up to see a woman emerge from the dark doorway. She was just about wearing a white Lycra jumpsuit, flared at the legs and slashed from neck to navel. The iridescent fabric fell loosely from her shoulders, barely masking her breasts, which seemed to me to be the fullest, yet most pert breasts I had ever seen. Her hips and thighs, sheathed by the sleek cloth and toned to perfection, were the shape and curve of which, in my pubescent state, I could only ever wish for.

Kimmy's eyes lit up like sparklers. I could tell by her face she'd found a new icon, and a wave of inadequacy hit me in the chest. I wanted to leave.

'Shit yeah, we'll be joining you,' Kimmy said, her shoulders still swaying in time to the music, her eyes now locked with those of the woman.

'Maybe we should come back another time,' I said, 'it's getting late.'

I was angry with her and I made no effort to disguise it. But I don't think she even noticed. The situation felt wrong and I yearned for the familiarity of my bedroom, to be anywhere other than here. I wondered if my parents had been in to check on me, if my mother was pacing up and down the kitchen, worried sick. My house felt like a million miles away.

'Oh you really should join us,' the woman in the doorway said, 'we're all having such a great time.'

I could almost feel the sleaze oozing toward me. It was more sex embodied by one person than I'd ever seen in my young life, and I didn't want to look at her anymore.

'Come on,' Kimmy said, her face pleading, 'don't be so boring.'

I looked at her for a moment and that was all the permission she needed. She grabbed my arm and led me in through the door. As I walked along the narrow entrance hall I passed uneasily close to the woman in white, and as I did so she lunged in towards me.

'Yes,' she breathed, 'don't be so *boring*.'

She scrutinized me as I walked by, her eyes running up and down the length of my body. Somehow she looked less beautiful now, but I put it down to the change of light, and was glad when we had some distance between us.

I looked back over my shoulder before descending the stairs, expecting to see her staring at me, but to my relief she had turned away. It looked as if she was closing and locking the door behind us but, although this did seem strange to me at the time, I walked on, choosing instead to ignore it.

The stairs curled down and round for several flights and I imagined they would lead us to a small venue below. However, when we reached the final turn what we saw was something else.

'Holy shit,' Kimmy said, 'check it out. How did I not know this place was here before? It's massive.'

The room was dark but vast, with a bar stretched along one wall. There was seating and tables around the edge, and in the middle a huge dance floor made up of illuminated squares in different colours. In the air hung a fog of tobacco smoke and Christ-knows what. It felt like I'd seen this place before, in a film, another decade, another life perhaps. *Retro* was right.

I was pleased we weren't the only people there, far from it. The place was nearly full, most of them centred on the dance floor; a sea of rocking and swaying bodies, captivated by the call of the music. It smelled of whisky and incense, a scent I can still conjure now if I ever want to punish myself that way.

Kimmy tapped my arm: she was going to the bar. She walked, I followed. I looked around at the other people in the room. Most of them wouldn't have been out of place in the seventies.

'Do you think it's fancy dress?' I shouted over the music, but Kimmy wasn't listening. She was working the barman, ordering us cocktails and, as often happened, I felt myself become invisible.

I saw her pull out a twenty pound note and wondered where from. Kimmy never had money. But the barman just smiled and waved it away. This struck me as odd but again, foolishly, I chose to ignore it. One day I would learn that nothing in life is free. But back then we were young, liberal with our optimism. Free drinks were free drinks and lessons relegated to the classroom.

The growling voice of some unseen deejay drifted out from the speakers, and The BeeGees became Tina Turner. Kimmy handed me a drink that seemed to be more fruit than anything else. I took a sip and nearly gagged, it tasted flammable, and the barman smirked as I put it down on the bar.

'Let's go dance,' Kimmy shouted in my ear, her eyes keen and wide, awaiting affirmation.

'I'll see what the next song is,' I said, which was an excuse and she knew it. I never was one for dancing, especially in front of other people.

'Fine,' she said, 'you stay here. I need to dance. Come and find me when you're ready to have fun.'

I watched her weave through the crowd, her walk becoming more of a strut the closer she came to the dance floor, while I shuffled myself onto one of the bar stools and tried to feel less disappointed in myself.

It was hot in the club, the atmosphere humid, charged. The hairs on my arms rose off the skin and the fillings tanged in my mouth. If we hadn't been so far underground I'd have sworn a thunderstorm was coming. I never did like thunder.

'You drinking that?'

I turned to see the barman.

'No,' I said.

'It'll help.'

'Help what?'

He didn't reply. Instead he cleaned lipstick off glasses with a cloth, holding them up to the light before placing them under the bar.

'You're going to be here a while,' he said, 'might as well make the best of it.'

I wasn't sure what made him think he knew how long I would or wouldn't be there. But then he looked over to Kimmy and I realised he was probably right.

Song after song Kimmy danced, while I sat, rooted to the bar stool, feeling more superfluous with every passing minute. I tried to remember why I'd climbed out my bedroom window in the first place, why I considered Kimmy such a friend, why being here was supposed to be better than being home, but I had nothing. That was the night I first learned the meaning of the word *toxic*. Long before Britney, Cosmo or agony aunts everywhere defined it for a generation I figured it out on my own.

'Was it your friend that brought you here?' the barman said after a while.

Yes, I wanted to say, *I'm her side-kick, her wingman, the proverbial Fat Friend. And you're quite right to pity me. I pity myself. You think she uses me? Well perhaps I use her too. Did you ever think of that, Mr Barman? Did you?*

But I didn't speak. I just sat, twirling the straw round in that heinous drink, wondering if I would ever in my life not feel ridiculous. It was too hot in here now. The ceiling felt lower, the air more compressed, pungent, contaminated almost.

'Most people come here to escape,' he said, 'but you look a little young for that.'

I looked over to Kimmy, still going for it, now with some sad, middle-aged man. *Age is irrelevant*, I thought, *running is running, however old you are*.

I was hot, much too hot.

'It's not me who needs to escape,' I said, stabbing the straw into the fruit in my drink, before finally pushing it away.

I needed to breathe so took off my cardigan.

After a moment the barman looked around, as if checking the area was safe, before speaking again.

'Then I suggest you leave,' he said, his tone now serious, covert even. 'Leave your friend and just go.'

I was stunned for a second, not sure I'd heard him right. I found the heat irritating, but the conversation more so. I turned to face him.

'Why would I do that?' I said.

'This place,' he said, 'it's not what you think. See them?'

He nodded to the dance floor and I turned to look. The dancing people now looked to be in a state of euphoria, their movements languid, less controlled, their faces tilted upward.

The pounding rhythm of the music was making my mind fuzzy. From somewhere a smoke machine hissed and belched out a vaporous cloud, blurring my view of the room. The deejay snarled something over the music, only adding to the confusion.

I blinked then turned back to the barman.

'They're just dancing,' I said.

'You sure about that?'

I wasn't, and I noticed he was no longer wiping glasses.

'I'll go and dance myself in a minute,' I said, my bravado transparent at best.

'No you won't.'

His bluntness shocked me. I had no comeback.

'I can see it in your eyes,' he said. 'You're an innocent, not like the others.'

He looked across the room then back at me, his face solemn, imploring almost.

'Listen to me,' he said. 'Forget your friend. There's no hope for her now. Save yourself and don't look back. When you get the chance *just run.*'

I thought he was going to say more, but before he could a man at the end of the bar called him over. I think maybe I saw fear in the barman's eyes as he walked away. But time has afforded my memory some artistic licence since that night, so I might not have seen any such thing at all. What I do know is he never returned, and I can only hope that wasn't a punishment for what he said to me.

As I tried to make sense of his words I looked around the room, somehow feeling watched. My eyes settled on an elevated glass booth in the corner, inside which was a man holding a microphone. From a distance he looked exceptionally tall, and something about his build was unnatural.

'Okay everyone,' the man in the booth said, 'if I don't see you all dancing by the end of this song there's gonna be trouble. And yes, *that means you.*'

He cackled over the end of the last track, while mixing in the next one. I watched as stragglers around the room made their way toward the main crowd on the dance floor. But I knew, despite what I'd said, nothing would make me get up there and dance.

I was unnerved by the barman. It may have been a wind-up, the talk of a crazy man, overworked and underpaid perhaps, but he sounded so sure. After I played the conversation over in my head a few times I decided – for me at least – the night was over; I would go and tell Kimmy I was leaving. So I headed in the direction of the dance floor.

I wiped beads of sweat from my top lip, planning just what I would say. For once I would be firm, make my own choices, and no amount of Kimmy's charm would change my mind. Not this time. And I almost believed it.

When I got to the edge of the dance floor I scanned the faces, but my view was obscured as arms and legs swung in rhythm to the music, groins thrust, heads rocked and bobbed. The room was one seething drunken mass and I wanted no part of it. The air now felt noxious as I breathed, and I wanted only to be outside, away from the chaos and noise.

Finally I spotted Kimmy, still gyrating around the middle-aged man. I called to her but she didn't hear. I shouted her name as loud as I could, but still no response, so I decided to fight my way through the crowd. But the moment I put my foot on the coloured panels of the dance floor my head started to spin, and I fell back towards the bar.

All at once my senses were heightened and I became acutely aware of the situation. I don't know why but I chose that moment to look for fire exits.

There were none. It registered that we were hundreds of people, deep underground, with only one, narrow, means of escape. An alarm bell rang in my head. And it rang loud.

I looked around and noticed by now I was the only person in the room not dancing. From the glass booth in the corner I thought I saw the towering silhouette of the deejay looking down at me, but it was dark and hazy so I couldn't be sure.

It was then I noticed others, in the shadows, dark shapes I could barely see. They hunched in corners, dozens of them, just out of view, quietly observing from a distance. Their beast-like posture disturbed me, and I was quite sure they hadn't been there earlier. I suddenly felt very afraid.

I saw the woman from upstairs slowly walking the perimeter, searching the darkness for strays, it seemed. On the other side of the room, a new barman had replaced the one that had spoken to me earlier. But this one didn't look anywhere near as friendly.

Fearful of standing out from the crowd I did my best to saunter back towards the dance floor, making my walk appear something like a dance. I wasn't sure why but I knew I didn't want to be the one person not dancing.

I felt obvious, unable to quite match the rhythm, but kept walking, somehow managing to keep my face neutral. When I again got close to the throng of dancers I swayed from side to side, attempting to copy the movements of those on the dance floor. It felt alien to me but I forced it, and when I looked up I could see the deejay had his back turned. I looked sideways and saw the barman had gone down the far end of the bar so seized the opportunity, calling up to the man dancing closest to me.

'Hey,' I said, in a kind of hushed shout, 'hey, you.'

But he didn't turn round. I checked I was still unobserved, then reached out and pulled on the man's shirt sleeve. When he again failed to respond I pulled even harder. This was enough to make the man turn his head.

'Can you call over to my friend?' I said. 'She's the one with the...'

But I didn't finish my sentence. The man couldn't hear me. His eyes were open but his face was comatose, his mouth hung wide like a fish on a slab. And yet he still danced.

I looked around at all the faces of the people dancing. Some were like the man, lifeless heads atop of somehow rhythmically animated bodies. While others bore manic smiles, wild eyes, as they lurched about to the music, the sweat pouring down their cheeks.

I caught sight of Kimmy, she was smiling; her eyes blank and staring, her movements beyond her own control. I thought I was going to throw up so swallowed down hard.

'That's just *wonderful*, people,' the deejay said, over the music, '*wonderful*.'

The dance floor heaved and throbbed. I tried to blend in to the edges without actually being a part of the whole.

'Just remember: this is where you belong. You were lost and now you're found, forever here, forever mine.'

I looked up towards the glass booth and saw the woman in white was now in there too. She was crouching down in front of the deejay and I watched as he closed his eyes.

'That's it, *feel the music…*'

I wanted to run but the fear of being seen held me in place. I looked at Kimmy and in that moment I hated her.

I looked over to the barman, who was still down the far end of the bar, then across the room to the stairs. It didn't look so far, not if I was quick. I took one last moment to check the glass booth, where the deejay was clearly distracted, and I knew what I had to do.

In that split second I took off and ran for the exit, not giving myself the option of working out the odds on the likelihood of escape. I took the stairs two at a time, stopping briefly at the turn to look back the way I'd come.

I saw Kimmy surrounded by the undulating horde of bodies on the dance floor. Her hips pumping back and forth, her arms reaching up for the glitter ball on the ceiling, her smile now so forced her eyes looked desperately sad in comparison.

Did she see me run away and leave her? I wondered if she was aware, if her synapses still fired away in her head despite her body doing its own thing. This thought horrified me then just as it does now. And it's a thought that, twenty-five years on, still keeps me awake at night.

But no sooner had I spotted Kimmy than I saw barman number two and the woman in white rushing across the room towards me. So, God forgive me, I ran. I ran up the stairs, all three flights, and down the narrow entrance hall, only stopping when I got to the door.

It was locked with slide bolts, three in all. Over my gasping breath I could hear footsteps pounding up the stairs toward me, and my hands trembled as I rattled the bolts open. The last one caught but I got it with a jerk, and the door swung open into the alleyway.

I fell outside and landed on my hands and knees in the dirt. I breathed in the night air and tried to stand, only to feel cold fingers wrap around my ankles and wrists, sharp nails digging into my skin.

My body flipped over, and my head hit the ground, as the man and woman pulled me up in a hog tie. I fought and pulled, and wriggled and squirmed, but with every move their grip tightened and I could feel them hauling me back inside.

I looked up at the fingers grasped round my wrists. They were no longer human. I looked up at their faces but it was dark and I could not trust what my eyes told me. They hissed and spat as I struggled for freedom, but they were strong and I could smell the incense, whisky and sweat, as they dragged me towards the door.

I thought of my mother, of the stupid row we'd had, and how I wished I'd not said a word of it. I wanted to be home now, away from this place, safe and warm in our rambling old house, with all its sticky windows and splintery floors. But more than that I wanted to be fifteen again, to have seen none of this, to have known nothing of this twisted adult world, and the horrors that lie in wait.

I was angry at my captors, I was angry at Kimmy for bringing me here, but most of all I was angry at myself for being too weak to stand up to all her bullshit. I felt the anger, the indignation, rise up inside until it had nowhere to go but explode clean out of me.

'No,' I screamed, 'you can't do this. Let me go. I'm not lost. I'm not running. Get your fucking filthy hands off me.'

'Shut up, little girl,' the woman said, 'you chose to enter, you belong to Him now. Just give in, or we'll have to hurt you.'

I think it was the fact she called me *little girl* that made me more angry than anything, and by sheer fury I managed to wriggle one of my legs free. I lashed out hard, catching the barman square in the groin. He stopped pulling on me and bent forward, as if waiting for the pain to subside.

I screamed as loud as I possibly could and kicked out with all the energy I had. As the barman struggled to regain his composure the woman reached down a skanky hand to cover my mouth. But I wouldn't let her. I continued to thrash about, yelling, her hand not able to make purchase on such a volatile target. So instead she reached around my throat, lifting my head and shoulders off the floor as she began to squeeze.

'You alright there love?' A voice called down the alley.

I felt myself hit the ground hard, and for a moment I was stunned. Through the haze I heard a door slam and realised, for the first time, I was alone.

I scrambled to my feet and limped towards the main high street. By the time I got to the end of the alley I was running. I ran towards the man that had called to me, the man that had probably saved my life. He was wearing one of those matching stag t-shirts, with what I can only assume was his name on the front. *Barry* it said. But I didn't stop to thank him. Instead I ran straight past him, through the town and all the way home. And not once did I look back.

My parents called the police but by the time they got to the alleyway *Disco Below* was gone. They said the doorway led only to an underground storage unit and there was no evidence to suggest the place had ever been used as an unlicensed dance club. They never found Kimmy.

I didn't go into town again and we moved away some months later. A kindness on the part of my parents, I think. One I'm not sure I deserved. The police pretty much left me alone after that. Except to tell me they'd found Kimmy's father at the foot of his stairs, neck broken, and did I know anything about that? Probably happened the same night, they said. Let us know if you hear from Kimmy, they said. And of course, in all the years since, I never did.

On good days I tell myself she would always have found a way to self-destruct; that her sad demise was inevitable given the downward trajectory of her short life. Other days I'm less forgiving of myself, and the internal accusations come thick and fast.

Sometimes I wake in the night, thinking I hear the clatter of sticks being thrown at my window. I lie in bed next to my sleeping husband, my eyes tightly shut, and I pray for the light of day. I tell myself I imagined it, that Kimmy's long gone. But I know if I looked down and saw her standing there, her mouth pulled up in that horrific smile, those wretched, dead eyes staring upward, I would lose what shred of sanity I still hold.

Then in the morning I reassure myself the children are still safe in their beds. I tell them I love them, that I will always love them. And when they've gone downstairs for breakfast I check the screws are still deeply sunk into their window frame; that no amount of tugging or heaving will force it to open. Only then can my day begin.

My children aren't much younger now than I was then, and I fear one day soon she'll come for them; that she'll entice them into helping her *dance the demons away*. But this time she won't get the chance. Not if I have to summon up the devil himself to drag her kicking and screaming back to the disco hell she clawed her way out of.

Rest in peace Kimmy, rest any way you want to. Just stay away from me and my family. You're not welcome here anymore.